For Amelie, Araba, Daniel, Jamie, Jude, Kate,
Matthew, Noah, Summer and William.
GL

For my grandparents.
RW

The Pink Bicycle

Gill Lobel

Illustrated by Richard Watson

THE PINK BICYCLE
TAMARIND BOOKS 978 1 848 53057 7

Published in Great Britain by Tamarind Books,
a division of Random House Children's Books
A Random House Group Company
This edition published 2011

1 3 5 7 9 10 8 6 4 2

Text copyright © Gill Lobel, 2011
Illustrations copyright © Richard Watson, 2011

Set in Baskerville Infant

TAMARIND BOOKS
61-63 Uxbridge Road, London, W5 5SA

www.**tamarindbooks**.co.uk
www.**kids**at**randomhouse**.co.uk

Addresses for companies within The Random House Group Limited can be found at:
www.randomhouse.co.uk/offices.htm
THE RANDOM HOUSE GROUP Limited Reg. No. 954009

A CIP catalogue record for this book is available from the British Library.

Printed and bound in China

Sunita loved her little red bicycle.
It had silver wheels with stabilizers
and it had a shiny bell.
The basket on the back was
just the right size for Blue Rabbit.

Blue Rabbit and Sunita went everywhere together.

He even had his own chair at mealtimes.

In the chilly winter
Blue Rabbit and Sunita
raced round and round the garden.

Ring-ting-a-ling went the silver bell,
while Blue Rabbit bounced happily in his special basket.

ring-ting
a-ling

Then one fine spring day
Sunita bumped her knee on the handlebars
and fell off.

"Oh, dear," said Mum,
"This bike is too small for you, Sunita!
We will get you a bigger one."

"But I don't want another bike!" said Sunita.
"Me and Blue Rabbit love this one!"

"Look, Mum. I can still ride my bike!" said Sunita.

But no matter how hard she tried,
her knees got in the way.

"Sunita, let's go to the bike shop," said Dad.
"Just to have a look."

"All right, just a look," said Sunita.

The shop window gleamed with a rainbow of bicycles.
Sunita looked. Dad looked. Sunita looked again. Then she saw it.
A sparkly pink bicycle, with lilac wheels
and a silver carrier on the back.
"Let's go in and try it," said Dad.

Bicycles!

OPEN

NEW BIKES INSIDE

10% OFF TODAY ONLY!!

"Perfect!" said Dad. "Just the right height."

"It's got no stabilizers!" said Sunita. "I will fall off!"

"No you won't," said Dad cheerfully. "I will help you. You will be riding in no time!"

"OK. I will try it," she said.

When they got home, Dad said,
"Come on, Sunita. Have a go?"

Sunita put Blue Rabbit in his special seat and climbed onto the saddle.
"OK," said Dad, holding the seat. "I've got you. Pedal away."

Sunita looked down at the grass. It seemed so far away!
"No," she said. "Blue Rabbit doesn't want to. I want to get off."

The next morning Dad wheeled the pink bicycle onto the lawn.
"Now," he said, "Just sit on the saddle
and let me push you
as far as the garden shed."

"You won't let go will you?" said Sunita.
"I won't let go," said Dad. "I promise!"

"OK," said Sunita.

She looked behind to make sure
Dad was holding on.

Dad gave a little push.

Suddenly the bicycle wobbled and tipped to one side.
"Now you've frightened Blue Rabbit!" she cried.

"Come on, Sunita," said Dad. "You were doing really well!"

But Sunita shook her head.
She sat behind the laurel bush with Blue Rabbit.

She hugged him and thought of all the happy times
they had together on the little red bike.
"I hate my new bicycle, I'm never going to ride it!" she cried.

The next day was warm and sunny.
"Just right for a picnic on Windmill Hill," said Mum.

"We will take the pink bicycle," said Dad,
"just in case you want to ride it."

Sunita hugged Blue Rabbit
and said nothing.

High on Windmill Hill a wild
wind roared through the trees.

They found a lovely spot at the top of a slope.

It was a wonderful picnic. There were samosas, crisps,
peanuts and popcorn, barfi and gulab jamun, rolled in coconut.
There was blackcurrant to drink.

mmm...

"Have some more samosa, Blue Rabbit!"
Sunita popped a bit in his mouth.

Suddenly a wild gust of wind caught Blue Rabbit,
and it whisked him down Windmill Hill.
Sunita screamed. She jumped to her feet.

Blue Rabbit rolled
head over heels
down
and down
the grassy slope.

He was heading for the stream!

Sunita grabbed the pink bicycle.
"Hang on, Blue Rabbit, I'm coming!" she yelled.
She jumped on and scooted down the grassy slope.

Over the buttercups
she bumped,
the wild wind
streaming
through her hair.

Suddenly, the slope levelled out and her feet found the pedals.
Push, push. She was off with hardly a wobble!

Down the sandy path she rode and there was Blue Rabbit, stuck in a bramble bush. "It's all right, Blue Rabbit, I've got you." Sunita gently pulled the brambles out of his fluffy pink ears.

ring-ting
-aling

She put him in the basket and pedalled all the way back up the hill,
the little bell ring-ting-a-linging joyfully.

OTHER TAMARIND TITLES
Written by Gill Lobel

For her birthday, Araba Rose's Gran gives her a magic hobbyhorse called Starlight. At night Starlight takes Rosie on wonderful journeys through the night skies, to the North Pole and under the sea.
Age 6+

Keisha has started her new school but misses her old friends. Sometimes she doesn't want to go. Then Keisha finds two dolls, Little Katy and Tiny Katy, and decides that they will be her friends. When Keisha loses her dolls at school, she finds out how many friends she truly has.
Age 5+

Joy rides at Penniwells Riding Centre. Ravi rides there too, but he never, ever talks. Joy worries about him. She doesn't know he's autistic. One day Joy needs Ravi's help.
Age 7+

For readers of *The Pink Bicycle*:

If you'd like to see the rest of our list,
please visit our website:
www.**tamarindbooks**.co.uk